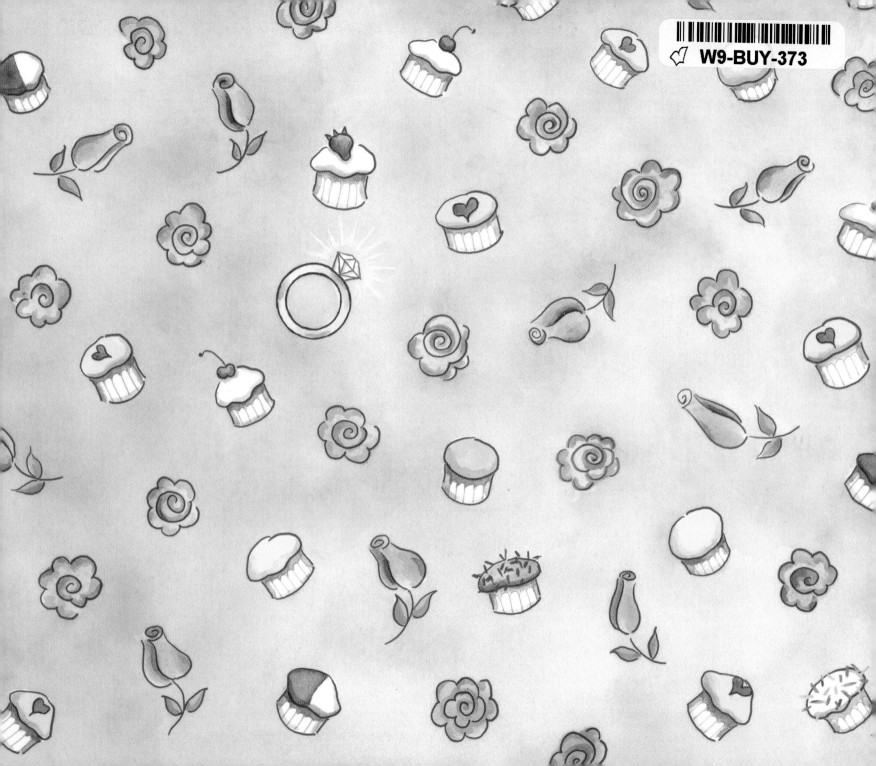

For Liesl, who pulls me along,

and for her father, who didn't drop the ring

Henry Holt and Company, LLC
Publishers since 1866
175 Fifth Avenue
New York, New York 10010
mackids.com

Library of Congress Cataloging-in-Publication Data
Géser, Gretchen.
One bright ring / Gretchen Géser. — 1st ed.
p. cm.
Summary: A little girl catches a ring as it falls from a man's pocket, then pulls her mother along
as she bravely pursues him past increasing numbers of obstacles trying to return his precious jewel.
ISBN 978-0-8050-9279-0 (hardcover)
[1. Stories in rhyme. 2. Lost and found possessions—Fiction.] I. Title.
PZ8.3.G33One 2013   [E]—dc23   2012021080

First Edition—2013
The illustrations for this book were created using watercolor, ink, software, and a digital stylus.

Printed in the United States of America by Worzalla, Stevens Point, Wisconsin.
3   5   7   9   10   8   6   4   2

One Bright Ring

GRETCHEN GÉSER

Henry Holt and Company

NEW YORK

NE big smile.

One little hole.

One bright ring

falls to the ground.

A bounce, a catch,
a girl shouts, "Hey!"
But two jackhammers
pound and smash.

And that one man
with one big smile
(and one little hole)
is gone.

A moment of thought.

Three tugs on Mommy's sleeve.

And one brave girl
follows one man
with one big smile
(and one little hole).

But four little babies

block the path.

One brave girl cries,

"This way! This way!"

And she pulls her mommy through.

Then five frisky dogs

spread out like a fan.

But one brave girl hollers,

"This way! This way!"

And she leads on . . .

. . . until she sees six signs

and comes to a STOP.

Left is school.

Right is a playground.

Straight ahead, a park with roses

and a bakery . . .

. . . with seven kinds of cupcakes
(at least).

"This way! This way!"
shouts one brave girl.

And she spies one man

with one big smile

(and one little hole)

with his love

among the roses.

And one brave girl

tiptoes eight soundless steps . . .

. . . while the man checks his pockets

nine frantic times.

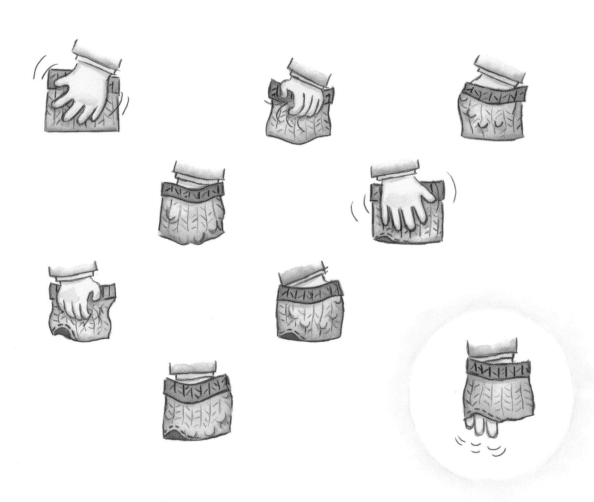

He searches the ground

and sheds ten small tears.

Then one brave girl

drops one lost ring

right under his nose.

And the man smiles one big, big smile.

And one brave girl cheers,

"This way! This way!"

and leads her mommy . . .

. . . to cupcakes.

(Twenty, at least.)

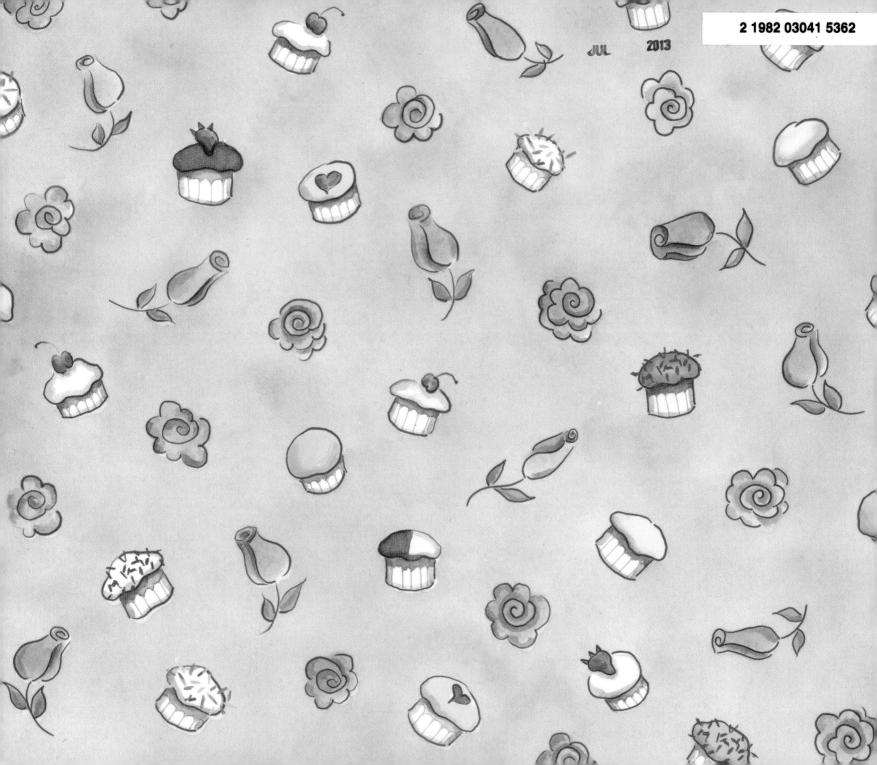